Princess Evie

Sarah KilBride
Sophie Tilley

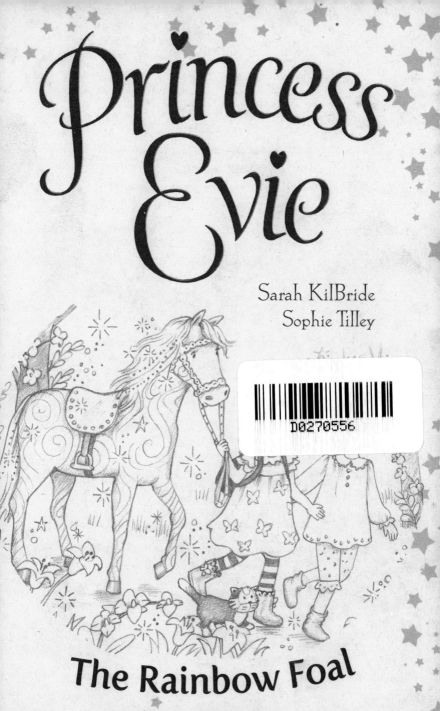

D0270556

The Rainbow Foal

SIMON AND SCHUSTER

CHAPTER 1

Sparkling Springtime

Princess Evie and her kitten, Sparkles, had been busy helping out with the spring-cleaning at Starlight Castle. The sun shone brightly through Princess Evie's gleaming bedroom windows and there wasn't a cobweb to be seen – quite an achievement, considering how high her room was! Evie opened her windows wide and the room filled with fresh spring air and birdsong. The sound of her ponies' neighs drifted in from Starlight Stables.

"Come on, Sparkles," said Evie. "I think it's time to do some spring-cleaning down at the stables."

Immediately, Sparkles stopped pouncing on a feather duster and was ready at the door. He always went to the stables with Evie, just in case they ended up riding through the tunnel of trees. You see, Evie's ponies weren't any old ponies. They were magic ponies and, whenever they went through the tunnel of trees, they took Evie and Sparkles on a magical adventure in a faraway land.

Together they raced down the grand staircase. It was lined with portraits of Evie's ancestors, sitting proudly on shining horses. Evie always stopped to look at one particular painting of a young girl on a pretty pony.

"I'm sure I can see the tunnel of trees in the background, Sparkles," said Evie.

Sparkles rubbed his cheek against Evie's ankle, and then skipped down into the great hall and out to the gardens.

Although it was sunny, there was

a strong breeze that blew white
clouds across the sky. Princess Evie
and Sparkles decided to walk across
the lawn and then take the short cut
through the orchard. It was looking
beautiful. Daffodils and crocuses
danced cheerfully in the wind and
green buds decorated the fruit tree
branches. Evie and Sparkles even
spotted a honeybee that had come out

into the spring sunshine to enjoy the flowers.

"Don't worry, busy bee," smiled Evie. "It won't be long before these trees are covered in blossom and then you'll have plenty of food!"

All the ponies at Starlight Stables neighed when they heard Evie's voice and saw she was on her way. They were always pleased to see her because Princess Evie was an important part of their family. Each pony loved Evie and had shared amazing adventures with her. Shimmer kicked her stable door as Evie walked into the yard.

"All right, my beauty," said Evie as she closed the gate.

She went to Shimmer's stable and smoothed her thick mane. Last winter,

Shimmer had taken Evie through the tunnel of trees to an ice cave where they had met an ice pixie called Freya. Evie always made the loveliest friends on her adventures, and that wasn't all – whenever they rode through the tunnel of trees, her ponies were magically transformed. Their coats became a completely different colour and their tack sparkled with decorations. Evie's clothes changed too. When Star, her Arab pony, took Evie to the desert, she found herself wearing an outfit of purple silk and a pair of sand slippers that curled up at the toes.

Star was in the stable next to Shimmer and, because it was such a fine day, Evie decided that Shimmer and Star should have some time in the

paddock. As soon as she turned them out, they rolled in the fresh grass and galloped around the field together.

"Right, Sparkles," said Evie. "Let's start with spring-cleaning our bridles."

Evie and Sparkles went into the tack room and collected some of her ponies' leather bridles. She carried them back into the sunshine and took them apart, making sure all the buckles were in good working order and the leather wasn't damaged in any way. She always cleaned her tack and made sure it was safe to use, but today Evie was going to oil it.

When tack became hard and dry, it was time to feed the leather with special oil. Evie got a clean cloth and poured a small amount of the oil out. She rubbed it into all the different parts of the bridles – the cheek pieces, the brow-bands, and the nose bands. Some of them were quite fiddly! It was a slow job but a very important one. If the leather wasn't supple it might snap and that could be dangerous for Princess Evie and her ponies.

While she worked on Star and
Shimmer's saddles, Evie watched the
ponies playing in the spring sunshine.
She wouldn't be able to ride either of
them for the next few days, because she
had to wait for the oil to be completely
absorbed before using their saddles
again. Shimmer and Star were good

friends and Evie could see how much fun they were having out in the warm sunshine together.

Sparkles was in the paddock having a chat with one of his favourite ponies, Indigo. She was a beautiful golden Haflinger pony with a white mane and tail. Although she was quite small, Indigo was strong. Sparkles was especially fond of her because she was gentle and, while she had lots of energy, she was never impulsive.

Indigo and Sparkles trotted over to watch as Evie finished cleaning the

tack and put everything back together.

"Would you two like to go through the tunnel of trees today?" asked Princess Evie.

Even though Sparkles was only a cat, Evie knew he could understand every word she said. As soon as he heard Evie mention the tunnel of trees, Sparkles miaowed and jumped onto the gate and into the yard. He followed Evie into the tack room, where she hung up the bridles and got Indigo's halter and the grooming kit. Before she could saddle her pony up, she would have to brush out Indigo's coat.

It always took a little longer at this time of year. All of Evie's hardy ponies – Silver the Welsh Mountain, Willow the New Forest and, of course,

Indigo, had spent the winter out in the fields. At the beginning of spring, they still had thick winter coats. Evie loved brushing this hair out to gradually reveal her ponies' beautiful summer coats. Their colours and markings became lighter and more defined; even the swirls and whorls seemed shinier. And it wasn't just Evie who loved the process of brushing out the ponies' winter coats. A row of sparrows and blue tits was already waiting on the stable roof for the soft hair that made a warm lining for their nests.

"Let's do some spring-cleaning with you Indigo," said Evie, tying her pony up.

Evie started by cleaning out her Haflinger's hooves. Then she brushed Indigo's golden coat with the dandy brush. When Evie had finished grooming there were clumps of hair blowing around the stable yard. The twittering birds that had been watching flew down from the roof and began to collect it.

As Evie tacked her pony up, the clouds darkened. Her ponies went to stand under the trees and in the field shelters.

"It looks as if there's going to be a spring shower, Sparkles," said Evie. "Come on, let's get our rucksack of useful things. If we're quick we should miss the rain."

Sparkles found Evie's rucksack hanging by Shimmer's hay net. They could never go through the tunnel of trees without it – there was always something in there that they needed on their adventure. Evie put on her rucksack and mounted Indigo. Sparkles jumped up after her, they were ready for an adventure. Evie loved riding Indigo. Haflinger ponies are quite light on their feet, and Indigo had a lovely balanced action. As soon as they were out of the stable yard, the first drops of spring rain began to fall. Indigo broke into a smooth canter and made her way across the fields, towards the tunnel of trees. "I wonder where the tunnel will take us today," said Evie.

CHAPTER 2

Rainbow Reunion

As soon as they came out of the tunnel of trees they saw a host of butterflies fluttering around them. Ahead of them was a shimmering rainbow and Evie knew exactly where it would lead them.

"Hooray!" said Evie. "We're going to the Rainbow Garden. I hope we're going to see Violet and all the other Rainbow Girls again."

Indigo whinnied and shook her long mane, which was now beautiful shades of pink. Her coat swirled and shone

and seemed to reflect all the colours of
the rainbow. Evie's flowing dress was
patterned like the butterflies' wings,
with pretty sleeves that quivered in the
breeze.

"Come on, Indigo," said Evie
happily. "I'm sure you can remember
the way!"

Without any hesitation, Indigo started to climb up the rainbow, following the delicate butterflies into the clouds. Soon they trotted out into the Rainbow Garden where, sure enough, Evie's old friend Violet was waiting for them.

"Oh Indigo, you clever pony!" said Violet, stroking the pretty pony's nose. "I knew you'd come back to see us. Well done for remembering the way!"

"Violet," smiled Evie, "it's so lovely to see you again."

Evie hopped down and gave her friend a hug.

"And you, Evie," said Violet. "I can't wait to tell the other Rainbow Girls that you're here."

Violet led them through the Rainbow Garden. The garden was blooming with

exotic flowers of every shape and size.
There were fragile orchids growing
in the trees, tall red lilies that looked
like flaming trumpets and pretty pink
mimosas with leaves that snapped
shut when you touched them. The
air was filled with the fragrance of
tiny jasmine flowers. As they walked

through the wonderful garden, the friends remembered their last adventure together.

"Do you remember the first time you saw this garden?" said Violet. "There were no colours in it at all!"

"How could I forget?" Evie replied. "I was so disappointed. Everything was grey – the flowers, the trees, even the lawns!"

Evie, Sparkles and Indigo helped to

return colour to the Rainbow Garden by collecting precious gemstones from each of the Rainbow Girls. When Evie put the gemstones into the magic well, the garden filled with rainbow bubbles and all the flowers returned to their beautiful shades.

"If you, Sparkles and your magic rainbow pony hadn't come to visit us, this garden would still be grey," said Violet. "You are a great team."

Towards the end of the garden they found Rosa's summer house, where all the Rainbow Girls were working hard. They were so busy that at first, no one noticed Evie and Violet arrive. Azure and Fern were cutting tiny petals from a huge piece of white silk. Magenta and Rosa were painting the edges of

the heart-shaped petals with the palest
of pinks, yellows and greens. Evie
could see Saffron and Amber in the
summer house making some food. It
smelled delicious!

It was Rosa who saw Evie first.
She put down her paintbrush and
ran over to give Evie a hug. It wasn't
long before all the Rainbow Girls
surrounded Evie, Sparkles and Indigo.

Rosa, Magenta, Saffron, Amber, Fern
and Azure were all chatting away at
once and welcoming them with smiles
and kisses.

"It's brilliant that you've returned,"
said Rosa.

"How fantastic that you've come
today, Evie," said Magenta as she gave
Sparkles a hug. "It's one of the busiest
days of the year."

"Today is the start of our Rainbow
Blossom Festival and we've got lots
of jobs to do before the festival can
begin," added Rosa.

"Come on Evie," said Amber, taking
Evie by the hand. "Let's sit down and
tell you all about it."

There was a cluster of rainbow-
coloured cushions underneath the apple

tree. Everyone got comfy, especially Sparkles who sat on Evie's knee and listened carefully to the Rainbow Girls.

"Every year, visitors come from far and wide to enjoy the beautiful blossoms in our Rainbow Garden," said Violet.

"But first we have to make the blossoms from this very special silk." said Rosa. She held up the material and the sun shone through it, making it shimmer.

"Azure and I have to cut each petal perfectly," said Fern. "It takes a lot of concentration."

"Then Magenta and I paint them," said Rosa.

"Just around the edges, so each petal has a hint of colour," added Magenta.

"My job is to prepare our pony, Corolla, and our chariot," smiled Violet. "She will take us through the air when it's time to sprinkle the trees with our beautiful blossoms."

"Then we can relax under the trees and eat our delicious picnic and sing flower songs," added Fern. "Just like everyone else!"

"It's Fern's and my job to prepare the feast," continued Azure.

"So you see," said Violet, "we could

do with an extra pair of hands and paws, and maybe even another set of hooves!"

"We'd be happy to help you," said Evie, "wouldn't we?"

Sparkles purred and Indigo neighed.

"Thank you, Evie," said Rosa. "We can always count on you."

"Will you come with me to the yard and prepare the chariot please?" Violet asked Evie. "It needs a good spring clean, and we'll have to give Corolla an extra groom as this is her special day."

"We'll have her ready in no time!" said Evie.

"Brilliant!" smiled Magenta. "We'll meet you down at the yard at midday."

CHAPTER 3

Scouring the Landscape

Evie and Sparkles mounted Indigo.

"Come on up, Violet," she said.
"There's room for the three of us."

Indigo trotted away, taking Evie,
Violet and Sparkles to the yard. It
wasn't far, and when they got there
Evie tied Indigo up and gave her some
fresh water and hay. Violet opened the
shed door and took her friend inside.
Evie gasped when she saw the chariot.
Even though the shed was gloomy,
she could see that the carriage was

decorated with rainbow jewels and had
wheels of silver.

"We only use this chariot for the
Rainbow Blossom Festival," said
Violet. "It needs a really good clean."

Together, Violet and Evie pulled the
chariot out into the sunlight. Even
though it was quite dusty, it was
beautiful.

The friends sorted through cloths,
brushes and sponges, and filled a
bucket with soapy water. Sparkles had
a lot of fun chasing the frothy bubbles,

while Violet and Evie swept and scrubbed and polished. They weren't just cleaning the chariot to make it look spectacular. They were cleaning it for the same reasons that Evie had to clean her tack, to make sure that it was in good condition and was safe to use. While the girls worked away, they checked all the nuts and bolts and oiled each moving part, making certain that everything was in good, working order.

"I cleaned the harness earlier this morning, but I think I may have to adjust some of the straps as Corolla has grown rounder this spring!" said Violet

Evie laughed. "Yes, some of my ponies get carried away at this time of year. I think it's all the fresh grass."

As Violet undid some of the silver

buckles and loosened the straps, Evie
looked at the gleaming harness closely.

"This doesn't look like any of the
driving harnesses I've seen before," she
said.

"That's because there's something
a bit different about Corolla," said
Violet with a smile. "She's got wings

and can fly through the air!"

"Like Pegasus!" said Evie. "I've read the myth in Starlight Castle's library, but I never thought I'd ever meet a winged horse."

"Well, today is your lucky day," said Violet. "She's a real beauty. You'll see when we get her in from the fields. And this year she's in such good condition, she's radiant. She's had a sparkle in her eyes for the past few weeks. I think she's been looking forward to today."

"I can't wait to meet her," said Evie. "I don't think Indigo can either."

Sure enough, Indigo sniffed the air and whinnied loudly, but there was no reply.

"She's probably too busy eating!" said Violet, polishing the silver wheel spokes. "She knows that it's her special day and she'll need lots of energy. We'll bring her in when we've finished here."

Evie brushed the dust off the gemstones and then washed them gently with a damp cloth. Finally, she polished each jewel with a duster until every facet shone magnificently.

Soon the girls stood back to admire their work. The chariot glittered in the spring sunshine.

"Amazing!" said Evie.

"You wait," said Violet. "It looks even more wonderful when Corolla is pulling it through the sky!"

Violet collected Corolla's halter and they made their way to the paddock. But when they arrived, there was no pony.

"That's strange," said Violet. "She normally waits by the gate when she hears me coming."

Evie scanned the field but could see no sign of the pony. Violet called her name and Indigo whinnied, but Corolla didn't appear. Evie could see that her friend was worried.

"Let's go in and have a good look," said Evie. "She can't have gone far.

Perhaps she's in her shelter or behind those trees."

Sparkles hopped through the gate, his whiskers twitching. Violet opened the gate and Evie followed her into the field. They walked to the shelter, calling Corolla's name. They looked behind the trees, but there was no winged pony.

"Could she have flown off to another field?" asked Evie.

"She has never done that before," said Violet. "Although, this morning she was very unsettled. She kept lying down, then getting up and walking around as if she was uncomfortable."

"Perhaps she was feeling nervous," suggested Evie.

"Perhaps," said Violet. "I'll get some food to rattle in a bucket. Hopefully she'll hear it and fly back here."

"Good idea," said Evie, smiling. "That usually works!"

While Evie waited for her friend, she called the pony's name again. Violet returned with the bucket of food and shook it loudly.

They waited for a few minutes,

hoping to hear the sound of Corolla's wings or perhaps a neigh, but there was nothing.

"We'll find her, Violet," said Evie quietly.

"I hope she's all right," said Violet.

The girls looked around the paddock, even though it was obvious that Corolla was not there.

"I'm sure she's OK," said Evie reassuringly, holding Violet's hand. "Ponies sometimes do strange things when they know something special is about to happen. She won't have gone far."

Violet tried to smile.

"Should we let the other girls know?" asked Evie.

"Let's go to the top of the field," said Violet. "We'll get a good view of the Rainbow Valley from there. If we can't see her then we'll have to send out search parties."

The girls, Indigo and Sparkles raced to the top of the fields. Violet was right, they could see for miles and it was breathtaking. Rainbows arched over the rolling green hills and small rainclouds hovered over parts of the valley. While the girls searched for Corolla, Sparkles played with the string of Evie's rucksack as if he was trying to untie it.

"Of course, Sparkles!" said Evie. "There must be something in here that

will help us." She opened up her
rucksack of useful things and the very
first thing that she pulled out was an
old brass telescope.

"Perfect!" said Evie. "Now we can
see even further."

She held the telescope up to her eye.
Where could Corolla be?

CHAPTER 4

Corolla's Special Day

Evie passed the telescope to Violet.

"Do you want to have a look? After all, you know what your pony looks like."

Violet took the telescope and moved it slowly along the horizon. Suddenly, she stopped and turned the lens slightly to focus.

"There she is!" she cried.

Evie and Violet cheered and Sparkles purred, while Indigo let out a happy whinny. Evie could see how relieved Violet was. "She's at the edge of Kaleidoscope Wood!"

"Is she all right?" asked Evie.

"I can't see. She's too far away."

"Indigo, we need you to take us to Corolla as fast as you can!" said Evie.

She jumped up into the saddle, followed by Violet and Sparkles.

"I'll tell you the way," said Violet, as Indigo broke into a gallop over the field.

Soon they were racing towards a gate. Indigo seemed to sense there was no time for the girls to dismount and open it so she leaped over it.

"That's it, Indigo," called Evie as the wind whistled past them. "We're almost there."

They raced along the slopes and were soon in the field that lay next to Kaleidoscope Wood. There, standing by the trees, was a dappled pony. As they got closer, Evie noticed her coat was similar to a blue roan pony's except, instead of it being a blue-grey colour, it was violet. Her wings were folded tightly against her body but Evie could see they sparkled with delicate markings, like a butterfly's wings. The most striking thing about this pony was how much she was sweating. Her mane was wet and her coat was dripping.

"Corolla," said Violet softly, getting down from Indigo.

Corolla took a step back. She was breathing fast and looked agitated. Her eyes were full of fear and she was letting out short, sharp neighs...

"We need to get help," said Violet. "I've never seen her like this before."

"I'll go," said Evie. "You stay with your pony, she needs you. Shall I go to Rosa's summer house?"

"No," said Violet. "This is serious. We need the vet, Ginny Martingale, she'll know what's wrong."

"Where will she be?" asked Evie.

"Just follow the stream to the bottom of the valley. Her cottage will be the first one you come to, it's next to the bridge."

"Be brave, Violet," said Evie, giving her friend a hug. "We'll bring Ginny back as quickly as we can and she'll help Corolla get better. Try not to worry, Corolla is a strong pony."

As Evie made her way on Indigo, she thought about what could be wrong with Corolla. Perhaps she had colic – she was showing all the symptoms. Or worse still, maybe she had eaten something poisonous. Whatever it was, the poor pony was in pain and a lot of distress.

It only took a few minutes for Evie, Indigo and Sparkles to arrive at the vet's cottage.

"Please, come quickly," said Evie, as

Ginny opened her front door.

"Whatever is the matter?" asked the vet.

"The Rainbow Girls' pony, Corolla, is sick," said Evie, trying to catch her breath. "She's sweating and I think she's in a lot of pain."

"Where is the poor thing?" asked Ginny as she grabbed her vet's bag.

"Violet is with her at the edge of the wood," Evie replied. "She's never seen Corolla like this before."

"Violet was right to send for me," said Ginny. "We need to get there quickly."

But they were too late. When Ginny and Princess Evie arrived at Kaleidoscope Wood they found Violet standing by Corolla, looking pale and shaken. Corolla looked brighter than the last time Evie had seen her. Her eyes shone and she stood calmly, whickering quietly. There was something else – Evie could see an extra set of very long, spindly legs.

Corolla moved slightly and Evie saw the most beautiful rainbow-coloured foal standing beside her. Its coat swirled and shimmered, and its fluffy mane and tail were the colour of sunsets. Although it had only been born a few minutes ago, it was already standing unsteadily and shaking its small wings. It looked up at its mother with bright eyes and, when it blinked, Evie noticed how long and sparkly its eyelashes were.

"Are you all right, Violet?" asked Ginny.

"I think so," said Violet, not sounding very sure.

"Perhaps Evie could look after you for a minute," said Ginny. "While I check mum and foal. They both look well but you can never be too sure."

Evie took Violet by the hand and led her to sit down on the soft grass.

"It all happened so quickly," said Violet. "One minute a pair of tiny hooves appeared and the next, there was this beautiful foal."

"It's a miracle!" said Evie.

"It explains why Corolla has been looking so well," smiled Violet. "And why she put on all that weight!"

"And it explains why she was behaving so strangely this morning," added Evie. "Well, you did say that today was her big day."

Ginny came over and sat next to the girls.

"Corolla and her foal are fine," said the vet. "Well done, Violet. Your pony knew you were there for her, in case something went wrong, but you helped her to give birth safely by standing back and not disturbing her. It's tough, and can be traumatic, but ponies

instinctively know what to do."

Ginny had given Corolla and her foal a check up, making certain that they were both healthy.

"The first twenty-four hours of the foal's life are the most important," she said. "They need to be able to stand in the first hour and feed in the second, that's when their bodies are able to absorb the most antibodies from their mother's milk."

They all watched as Corolla's foal began to suckle. Corolla was gently whickering and sniffing her baby's coat.

"It looks like Corolla is going to be a great first-time mum," smiled Ginny. "She's bonding with her baby and connecting with her through all the

senses. Her foal's senses will develop
fully over the next couple of weeks."

"Do some ponies not bond with their
foals?" asked Evie.

"You have to watch new mums
carefully. Sometimes their maternal
instinct isn't very strong, or they may
still be suffering after giving birth,"
said the vet. "But it's important not to

interfere with the first contact unless you have to. All these two need now is to be alone, to bond and recover."

The friends looked at each other, sharing the same thought.

"Corolla won't be able to draw the Rainbow Blossom Chariot this year, will she?" asked Violet.

"I'm sorry, but that's completely out of the question," smiled Ginny. "She needs time to rest."

"Of course, she's exhausted after delivering her foal," said Evie. "But what are we going to do for the Rainbow Blossom Festival?"

"I think I have an idea who could pull the rainbow chariot for us," said Violet, gazing at Indigo. "What do you think, Evie?"

Evie guessed what her friend was thinking and smiled. Indigo stopped munching the grass and looked up at the girls. She blinked at them as if she knew what Evie was going to say next.

"Indigo," said Evie. "How would you like to pull the Rainbow Blossom Chariot this year?"

CHAPTER 5

Petals Away!

"Has Indigo ever drawn a carriage or a cart before?" asked Violet.

"We had a go once and she enjoyed it," said Evie. "Haflingers are known to be good driving ponies but they certainly aren't known for flying through the air!"

"Don't worry," smiled Violet. "With a little help from the Rainbow Girls and the rainbow butterflies, Indigo will be perfect."

Evie looked up and saw that the sun was high in the sky.

"We haven't got much time," she said. "It's midday already."

"She's right, Violet," said Ginny. "You must go – after all, you can't delay the Rainbow Blossom Festival. I'll keep an eye on Corolla and her foal. They should be fine now."

Indigo took Evie, Violet and Sparkles back to the yard where all the Rainbow Girls were waiting for them with their baskets of delicate blossoms. They had had no idea why Corolla wasn't harnessed and ready to take them through the sky.

The girls were amazed and overjoyed to hear the news that Corolla had safely delivered a rainbow foal.

"It's so exciting!" said Rosa. "A new foal, born on the day of the Rainbow

Blossom Festival."

The Rainbow Girls couldn't wait
to meet the new addition but first
they had a very important task – to
prepare Indigo for the sprinkling of
the blossoms. Evie and Violet carefully
harnessed Indigo and adjusted the
straps so that it fitted her perfectly.

"Now all you need is a pair of

wings!" smiled Violet, stroking Indigo's mane. "It won't hurt at all, but it will take some magic."

Sparkles' whiskers trembled and Evie let out a gasp when they heard this. The Rainbow Girls stood around Indigo and without a word they reached into their pockets and took out their precious stones. The stones glittered and glowed in the spring sunshine. Violet whispered into the pony's ear and then placed her sparkling amethyst in Indigo's browband. Next, Rosa whispered something to Indigo and placed a dazzling ruby into her band. Evie wasn't sure what the Rainbow Girls were saying to her pony, but Indigo listened intently.

When the final jewel had been placed

into Indigo's bridle, the Rainbow Girls
held hands in their circle and looked
up to the sky. A swirl of rainbow
butterflies fluttered and spiralled
around Indigo until they almost hid her
from view. All that Evie and Sparkles
could see was Indigo's calm face.

When the butterflies stopped
spiralling and flew away, Evie and
Sparkles were astounded by what

they saw. Indigo stood proudly with
the most magnificent pair of butterfly
wings, with shimmering pink swirls
and pale yellow whorls. Indigo shook
herself and stretched her wings out
in the sun. Evie saw that around the
edge of each wing were tiny amethysts,
rubies and other twinkling gemstones.

"Hooray!" said Violet. "We did it!

What a gorgeous rainbow pony you
are, Indigo."

Evie ran over and gave her beautiful
pony a big hug and a stroke.

"Come on, girls," said Rosa. "We've
no time to lose!"

Violet and Evie attached the chariot
to Indigo's harness. They gave Indigo a
few minutes to get used to it and then

carefully loaded up the chariot with the baskets of delicate blossoms. Finally, they were ready to go.

"All aboard!" said Rosa, smiling.

Everyone climbed into the chariot and took their positions. Violet held the reins at the front of the chariot and made sure there was enough room for Evie beside her. Sparkles was feeling a bit nervous, so he snuggled up into Evie's arms.

"All right, Indigo," called Violet. "You know what you to do. Just take your time and you'll be fine."

Indigo walked out of the stable yard into the field where all the butterflies were waiting. She broke into a fast trot and, when she moved to a smooth canter, Evie realised that her hooves were no longer touching the ground. Indigo was flying!

The butterflies fluttered around the Rainbow Garden and the chariot followed silently, pulled along by the magnificent Indigo. Evie and Sparkles looked out and saw they weren't too high in the sky.

"Here's the first tree coming up!" called Rosa. "It's an apple!"

Magenta passed around the basket of creamy blossoms with a touch of

yellow around their frilly edges, and
everyone took a handful.

"On the count of three," called
Rosa. "One, two, three!"

Everyone opened their hands and
let the blossoms flutter down. When
the blossoms landed on the apple tree,
they magically attached themselves to
the branches, making the tree come to
life with the promise of spring. The
next tree was a cherry tree. Everyone

sprinkled it with blossoms that were painted with different shades of pink.

"I can't wait to come back at the end of the summer and see all the cherries," said Rosa as they flew on to the next tree.

Violet turned to Evie. "Would you like to have a go at driving Indigo?"

"Do you think I could?" asked Evie.

"Of course," said Violet, smiling. "You and Indigo are a great team."

Evie took the reins and immediately felt Indigo's power. Her wings were beating rhythmically and with every beat, Evie could feel the chariot being pulled further through the air. The butterflies were guiding Indigo, so all Evie had to do was let her pony know that she was there for her.

CHAPTER 6

What's in a Name?

They flew around the Rainbow Garden, decorating each of the trees with their beautiful, handmade blossoms, and soon the garden was complete.

Evie and Sparkles loved flying through the air with the Rainbow Girls. The fresh spring air made Sparkles' fur tingle and Evie's cheeks turn rosy.

"This is amazing!" laughed Evie.

"Indigo is a fantastic at pulling this chariot," said Violet. "And she looks as if she is enjoying herself too."

Violet was right. Indigo's ears were forward and she held her head up high as her rainbow mane flew out behind her. Princess Evie felt very proud of her.

"It's time for us to land now, Indigo," called Violet. "But don't worry, the butterflies will guide you."

Evie felt her pony descend as the butterflies led them to a clearing in the garden. Indigo's wings slowed down and soon she was trotting through the grass. Everyone cheered as she came to a halt.

"That was a perfect landing," said Rosa, opening the chariot's door and helping everyone out.

Saffron and Fern took a large picnic basket out of the chariot and together the Rainbow Girls laid out the special feast.

"I should think you're hungry after all that flying, Indigo," said Violet as Indigo tucked into the grass. "You're probably thirsty too. We'll get you some fresh water."

Violet and Evie went over to the garden's magic well and pulled out a bucket of fresh, clear water. The friends released the chariot from Indigo's harness and loosened some of the straps so the pony could relax.

They walked over to the picnic rug, which was spread out beneath a fluttering cherry tree, and joined Sparkles. He was sitting with the Rainbow Girls and already enjoying some special kitten biscuits.

"What a feast!" said Evie when she saw all the plates of delicious food that Saffron and Fern had prepared.

"Help yourself!" said Saffron.

"There's plenty for everyone."

Evie took a plate and filled it with an assortment of scrumptious sandwiches and delicious dips, as well as passion-fruit parcels and tasty tarts filled with tiny apricots and almonds. Saffron and Fern poured everyone a glass of rose-petal lemonade. Then Rosa and Violet stood up.

"We would like to propose a toast

to Princess Evie, Sparkles and Indigo," said Rosa.

"We'd like to thank you for coming back to the Rainbow Garden, Evie," added Violet. "And especially for helping to save our special day!"

All the Rainbow Girls raised their glasses and toasted Evie, Sparkles and Indigo.

"It's certainly been an adventure!" laughed Evie. "Perhaps we should toast the health of Corolla and her foal too."

"Of course!" agreed Rosa.

Everyone raised their glasses of rose-petal lemonade and wished Corolla and her newborn foal good health.

"We'll have to think of a name for the foal," said Violet.

"I know," said Magenta. "How about Blossom?"

"Or perhaps Kaleidoscope!" added Rosa.

"That's a lovely name, but it might be too long," said Violet. "We could call her Cherry."

"Or Rainbow," suggested Azure.

The Rainbow Girls had lots of ideas and the discussion continued as the girls tidied up the plates and the remainder of the picnic. Sparkles, bored by all this, played with a heart-shaped petal that had floated down from a branch above. A gentle breeze blew it out of his paws' reach each time he got close to catching it. After a few minutes of chasing, the pretty petal landed on his nose.

Violet and Evie began to giggle when they saw his cute little petal-nose. The other Rainbow Girls turned to see what was so funny.

"That's brilliant, Sparkles!" said Violet. "We could call the new foal Petal."

Everyone agreed that the name Petal was just right.

"What a clever cat you are, Sparkles," said Evie, giving her kitten a big hug and blowing the pretty petal away.

"I think we should have the naming ceremony before you go," said Violet.

"What an excellent idea!" said Rosa.

CHAPTER 7

Rainbow Wishes

Before they went to the field on the edge of Kaleidoscope Wood, the girls made little crowns and garlands using the pretty blossoms that were left over in the baskets.

Evie and Violet took off Indigo's harness. They wove cherry blossom into her mane and draped a garland of peach blossom around her neck. Rosa even made Sparkles a crown of tiny hawthorn blossom. Everyone looked beautiful, and soon they were ready to see Corolla and Petal.

When they got to the yard, Violet
went to the feed shed and got Corolla a
scoop of oats to keep her strength up.
Ginny took them to see the mare and
her new foal. The rainbow foal's coat
shimmered and Corolla looked content.

"They are doing really well," the vet
smiled.

"We've come to perform a naming

ceremony, Ginny," said Violet. "Would you help us?"

"Of course," said Ginny. "What have you decided to call her?"

"Petal," said Violet.

"Sparkles chose it," said Rosa.

"What a pretty name," said Ginny. "It's perfect for such a pretty foal."

The little foal was very inquisitive when she saw the Rainbow Girls and was especially interested in Sparkles. They touched noses and Sparkles purred while Petal whickered. Corolla was pleased to see everyone and neighed happily when Violet gave her the bucket of oats. Evie gently draped a garland of blossom around Corolla's neck and tucked a little spray of flowers into Petal's mane. Now they were all ready for the ceremony.

Everyone stood around Corolla and
Petal and, as if by magic, a rainbow
appeared above them.

"We are here today to celebrate the
safe arrival of Corolla's foal," said
Ginny. "A foal is full of promise and
each one of us here will help to take
care of her and love her. We give her

the name Petal and will each give her a wish for her future."

"Petal, I wish you happiness in the Rainbow Kingdom," said Violet.

"Petal, I wish you fields full of fresh grass," said Rosa.

"Petal, I wish you many safe journeys through the sky," said Magenta.

Princess Evie hadn't been sure what was going to happen but, after listening to Violet, Rosa and Magenta, she realised what she had to do.

She looked at the little foal and
thought about all the amazing
things that had happened that day.
She thought about returning to the
Rainbow Garden to see her old friends,
about finding the foal, and about
Indigo pulling the jewelled chariot
through the sky.

"Petal, I wish you many, many
wonderful adventures shared with
friends."

Each of the Rainbow Girls and
Ginny gave Petal a wish, while Corolla
looked proudly on.

"We'd better take Corolla and Petal
back to the shelter by the yard," said
Violet, when they had all finished. "It
looks as if it's going to rain soon."

A dark cloud moved slowly towards
them.

"I think it's time to make our way back to Starlight Stables," said Evie. "Indigo could do with some rest after today's excitement – we all could!"

Sparkles rubbed up against Evie's ankle and miaowed.

"Thank you, Indigo, for coming back to see us," said Rosa, stroking Indigo's rainbow mane. "And for pulling our chariot through the sky. You saved the day!"

"Well done, Sparkles, for choosing the perfect name for Corolla's foal," said Ginny, as she cuddled the kitten.

"And thank you for helping me with Corolla," said Violet, giving Evie a big hug.

"That's what friends are for," smiled Evie. "We promise we'll come back to visit you as soon as we can."

"We'd love to see you all soon," said Violet. "You must come back for next year's Rainbow Blossom Festival. Corolla and Indigo could pull the chariot together."

Everyone waved as Indigo trotted off to the tunnel of trees. They didn't have far to go because the tunnel was just in Kaleidoscope Wood. Princess Evie knew that Indigo's beautiful wings would disappear when they came out of the tunnel and were back at Starlight Stables. She stroked them one last time.

"You are a very beautiful rainbow pony Indigo," said Evie.

Indigo shook her mane and happily went into the tunnel. When they came out, her coat had returned to its beautiful gold and, of course, her wings had disappeared.

All of Princess Evie's ponies called out to them, welcoming them back to the stables. Evie took off Indigo's tack and groomed her, checking her for any strains or injuries.

"Well done," said Evie. "You worked hard today. You are such a strong pony – and a magic one too!"

Indigo nuzzled up to Evie. She loved going through the tunnel of trees and having adventures with Evie and Sparkles.

When Evie turned her Haflinger pony out into the paddock, Indigo rolled on the ground and then trotted around the field with her friends Silver and Willow. Evie and Sparkles went into the tack room to hang up Indigo's bridle and saddle.

"We'll have to carry on with our spring-cleaning tomorrow, Sparkles," said Evie. "There's lots more tack to oil, but I'm just too tired to do it today."

Sparkles was sitting by the hook

for Indigo's bridle, looking up at
something that was hanging from it.
Princess Evie carefully put Indigo's
tack down and went over to see what it
could be.

"Well I never!" she said, smiling.
"It looks as if Indigo is going to have
lots of fun this spring. It's a driving
harness, Sparkles!"

Evie took the harness down carefully.
It was beautiful, with silver buckles
and tiny gemstones sparkling along the
reins.

"Thank you Rainbow Girls," said Evie. "What an unforgettable day."

Evie and Sparkles made their way back to Starlight Castle. They decided to walk through the fruit orchard and, as they did, they noticed something amazing.

"Look, Sparkles!" said Evie, pointing up the branches.

All the trees were covered with fluffy blossoms.

"Miaow," said Sparkles as he began to chase a pink cherry-blossom petal that was floating on the spring breeze.

"I'm sure they weren't there this morning," laughed Evie. "I think that the springtime magic has really started!"

Pony Facts
&
Activities

Evie

LIVES AT:
Starlight Stables

FAVOURITE PONY:
Impossible to choose!

FAVOURITE PASTIME:
Going on adventures
with my magic ponies

FAVOURITE FLOWER:
Violets

FANTASY FOOD:

Apple-blossom ice cream

Indigo

BREED:
Haflinger pony

FEATURES:
Very strong, quick learners, very friendly,
driving ponies

HEIGHT:
From 13 hands to 15 hands

COLOUR:
All shades of chestnut with light-coloured
manes and tails

Horse Tack

Tack is the name for all the equipment you use with a pony. Can you guess what the piece of equipment is from the description?

1. The rider sits on this
2. This goes in the mouth and is connected to number 4
3. The rider holds these in their hands and uses them to steer the pony
4. This goes over the head of the pony and connects numbers 2 and 3
5. The rider's feet go into these
6. This sits under number 1 to protect the pony's back

ANSWERS: 1. SADDLE 2. BIT 3. REINS 4. BRIDLE 5. STIRRUPS 6. SADDLE PAD

Wordsearch

Now can you find those answers in this grid. They can be read forwards, backwards, diagonally, horizontally or vertically.

E	R	Q	B	I	T	S	V	C	X
L	L	G	M	T	H	A	E	T	E
D	M	D	R	H	U	D	H	B	S
I	R	B	D	K	H	D	S	N	Y
R	Z	B	W	A	L	L	I	C	I
B	V	P	Q	W	S	E	S	O	H
T	A	Z	A	Q	R	P	H	S	L
R	Q	R	X	L	U	A	X	H	I
I	C	R	W	B	B	D	K	R	T
S	P	U	R	R	I	T	S	X	P

Birthstones

The Rainbow Girls each have a special magic stone that they to help Indigo fly. Every month has a specific stone associated with it. Which one is your special stone?

January – Garnet
This red stone is a symbol of love and compassion

February – Amethyst
This pretty purple stone is said to help people have pleasant dreams

March – Aquamarine

This stone is often a pale blue-green colour and can help encourage bravery

April – Diamond

These very expensive stones are beautifully clear and sparkly.
They are often used in wedding or engagement rings

May – Emerald

A beautiful green colour, these stones are quite rare and are said to bring wisdom if you wear them

June – Moonstone

A very lucky stone that is supposed to bring good fortune! These stones are a milky-white colour although they can look almost blue

July – Ruby

Another beautiful red stone, these are often used to protect against bad dreams

August – Peridot

This stone is quite unusual but is a very pretty green colour. It is supposed to help bring happiness to the wearer

September – Sapphire

This stunning blue stone helps you to think through difficult problems

October – Opal

These can be lots of different colours and often look transparent.
It's often described as a stone of inspiration and creativity

November – Topaz

A pretty yellow stone that is said to be a symbol of love and affection

December – Turquoise

This stone is bright blue and a symbol of friendship and peace

Butterfly Cakes

The Rainbow Garden butterflies helped guide Indigo through the trees in the blossom festival. Try this recipe for some yummy butterfly cakes and see if you can make your cakes as pretty as the butterflies in the festival.

Remember to be careful when using an oven – always ask a grown-up to help you!

Ingredients for the cake:

100g butter

100g caster sugar

2 large eggs

100g self-raising flour

1 tsp vanilla extract

1 tbsp milk

To make the cakes:

1. Preheat your oven to 190°C/Gas Mark 5 and line a muffin tin with paper cases

2. Mix the butter and sugar until it's pale

3. Add the eggs and 1 tbsp of flour and mix

4. Mix in the flour, vanilla and milk then divide the mix evenly through the cases

5. Place the cakes in the over for 15-20mins until they are golden brown

6. Once they are cool cut a circle out of the top of the cakes, keep the tops to one side as you'll need them later

7. Scoop out a bit of the cake from the middle and fill the hole with buttercream

8. Cut the sliced tops in half and arrange them on top of the buttercream to look like wings

Ingredients for the buttercream icing:

140g butter

280g icing sugar

1-2 tbsp milk

To make the buttercream:

1. Beat the butter until it's soft
2. Then add the icing sugar and 1 tablespoon of the milk until the mixture is smooth

You could use food colouring to make the cakes and icing look extra pretty!

Pegasus Facts

Corolla is a very different type of pony to Evie's, as she has wings! The most famous winged pony was Pegasus, who appeared in Greek myths. He was said to be a beautiful winged horse and the son of Poseidon, the god of the Sea. There were many stories told about him but one of the most famous was that he became the great friend of the

King of the Gods, Zeus. They were such good friends that Zeus turned Pegasus into a constellation of stars so that he could live forever. Pegasus was supposed to have many magical powers including stopping a mountain from growing any taller by kicking it. As a friend of Zeus he also carried his thunderbolts through the sky.

Look out for more of Princess Evie's magical adventures . . .

at a bookshop near you!

Sarah KilBride ★ Sophie Tilley

Princess Evie

Fabulous free poster inside!

and the Forest Fairy Pony